The CLIMBERS

For the kids with love in their hearts and
courage in their bones – Ali

For Iris and Mathis – Alette

First American Edition 2019
Kane Miller, A Division of EDC Publishing

Text copyright © Ali Standish, 2019
Illustrations copyright © Alette Straathof, 2019

First published in Great Britain in 2019 by Stripes Publishing Ltd,
an imprint of the Little Tiger Group.

For information contact:
Kane Miller, A Division of EDC Publishing
P.O. Box 470663
Tulsa, OK 74147-0663

www.kanemiller.com
www.edcpub.com
www.usbornebooksandmore.com

Library of Congress Control Number: 2018958208

Printed and bound in China
STP/1800/0246/0419

2 4 6 8 10 9 7 5 3 1

ISBN: 978-1-61067-898-8

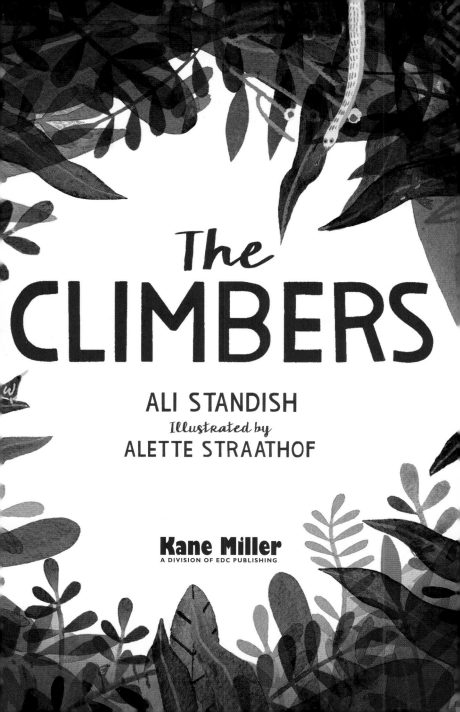

The
CLIMBERS

ALI STANDISH

Illustrated by
ALETTE STRAATHOF

Kane Miller
A DIVISION OF EDC PUBLISHING

Alma reached up.
Just a little farther and
she would be high enough
to see for miles.

"Alma!" called a voice.

She swung around to see her uncle standing below.
"Get down from that tree!" he shouted.

Alma sighed.
She had been so
close to the top.

"What were you doing?"
her uncle asked, taking
Alma's arm and leading
her back to their cottage.

"I just wanted to
see the forest,"
Alma said.

Alma had lived with her stern uncle ever since she could remember. But deep down, she never felt she belonged in the narrow town where they lived. She wasn't sure where she *did* belong. Only that there had to be more to the world than this.

Her uncle shook his head. "How many times must I tell you?" he huffed. "The forest is full of fearsome beasts. That's why only the hunters are allowed there."

Alma had heard this many times —
from her uncle, from her teachers, and
especially from the mayor.

When Alma peered into the trees, she
saw flashes of bright colors and heard
birds whistling songs that made her
heart feel like it had wings, too.

But all the townspeople seemed to hear was
the mayor's booming voice. All they saw
was his shaking fist.

"What's *beyond* the forest, Uncle?" asked Alma.

"The mountains," he said. "The settlers there are as bad as beasts themselves. They are so wild they even grow fur."

Alma sighed. She had heard this before, too.

"That's why you must stay here, safe in the town," said her uncle, handing her a broom.

The hard lines around his mouth faded. "It's for your own good, Alma. There's nothing beyond the town worth seeing."

Alma began sweeping the cottage steps. Her feet were on the ground, but her mind was still high up in the tree.

How could you know something wasn't worth seeing if you had never seen it? And if the world beyond the town was so terrible, why did she want to explore it so badly?

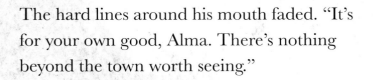

After supper that night, Anna lay in bed until she could not lie still anymore. Then she crept outside and stood in the yard, staring through the trees until she could not stand still anymore.

Then she set off running.

She had to see the forest for herself.

The forest air was cool.
The dancing trees were silver. Moonlight dappled the ground like pearls scattered from a string. There were flowers with a thousand petals that smelled of juicy plums. Yellow lizards slept in the trees.

Deeper and deeper Alma walked.
Birds sang carols all around her.
Their songs made her feel welcome.

Then she heard a
different sound. A cry.

Alma began to feel afraid.
She hid behind a thorny
thicket and peeked out into
the clearing ahead.

At first she thought the white
thing might be a fallen star. It was
huddled in a patch of ferns.

Then she saw a set of paws below
it. And a pair of eyes above.

Alma tiptoed across the clearing.
The crying thing was not a fallen
star. It was not a fearsome beast,
either.

It was a frightened bear cub!

"Hello," said Alma. She kneeled
down and stroked the cub. "You
must be from the mountains!
Are you lost?"

The bear was skinny and alone.
Alma couldn't leave him there where
hunters might find him.

So, snuggling the cub in her arms,
she ran back through the forest.

"I can't bring you home," she whispered. Her uncle would never allow a bear in the house. "But I know just the place."

She took the bear to an old shed at the edge of town. No one ever went there, so the cub would be safe. Alma took off her blanket and wrapped him up in it.

"Sleep now," she said. "I'll bring food tomorrow."

Then she ran home, slipped into her own bed and fell deeply asleep.

*

The next morning, Alma rose with the sun. As soon as she could escape from her uncle's watchful eye, she ran to the shed with cream and berries left over from breakfast.

The bear cub lapped up the cream.
The berries stained his white star
purple. He licked Alma's hand
to say "thank you."

"You're welcome," Alma said, giggling. "I should give you a name, too. How about Star Bear? What do you think?"

In her arms, the cub snored in agreement. He had fallen fast asleep.

*

Every morning, Alma brought Star Bear milk and whatever she could sneak away from her uncle's table. While Alma was at school, the bear slept in the shed.

Every night when the moon rose, they slipped into the forest to explore.

They splashed
under waterfalls.

They played hide-and-seek among the ferns.

They even climbed up the tall trees
and sat atop them. They ate sweet fruits
and stared at the distant mountains.

Soon Alma and Star Bear
were best friends.

"I'm sorry you got lost, Star Bear,"
said Alma one night. "But I'm
glad we found each other."

Star Bear grew bigger, until he was not a cub any longer. Although he was much larger than Alma, he was as gentle as a kitten when they played. Sometimes they fell asleep together in the clearing where Alma first found Star Bear. Alma felt warm and safe curled against his fur.

One morning, Alma was on her way to school when she heard voices in the square. A crowd was gathering around the mayor, who stood on the steps of the town hall.

Alma found her uncle. "What's going on?" she asked.

"The butcher's wife says she saw a bear last night," he said.

Alma's heart filled with worry. Had she and Star Bear been seen on their way back from the forest?

"What did the bear look like?" she asked.

"It was a giant beast," said her uncle, "with long, sharp teeth. Someone must have led it here."

"The mountain settlers!" cried the butcher's wife. "They led that beast here to eat us all up!"

"They want this town for themselves!" added Alma's uncle.

Alma wanted to tell them the truth, but she was afraid. If she told them about Star Bear, what would they do to him?

Just then the mayor spoke. "We must protect ourselves!" he shouted. "We will search for the beast. And we will build a timber fence around our town to keep these outsiders from coming in."

A great cheer rose up. Alma turned away. She had to get to Star Bear before the townspeople did!

Alma led Star Bear deep
into the forest.

"You will have to stay here," she
said, stroking Star Bear's nose.
"The shed is too dangerous now.
I'll come back when it's safe."

As Alma ran home, she heard a loud cracking sound. In the distance, she could see men chopping down the beautiful trees where she and Star Bear liked to climb.

The next day, they started to build the fence.

Every day, it grew higher and thicker. Every day, more trees disappeared from the forest. Every day, the mayor yelled for even more to be cut down. "The fence must be stronger!" he insisted.

Every night, Alma visited Star Bear. "They keep cutting trees," she said. "What will we do if they reach you? Or when the fence is finished? I won't be able to get out, and you won't be able to come in!"

It wasn't only trees that disappeared from the forest. So did the sweet fruits that grew from their branches. So did the yellow lizards and the singing birds that lived under their leaves. So did the shy forest deer that ate their bark.

The hunters began to come back without any food. The town grew loud with the sound of rumbling bellies.

Still the mayor ordered more trees cut down.

Before long there would be no forest left.

"We must tell them the truth," Alma said to Star Bear one night. "If the mayor knows you weren't sent by the mountain settlers, maybe he will stop cutting trees. If the townspeople see how gentle you are, maybe they will love you like I do."

The very next morning, Alma rode into the town on Star Bear's back. She trembled with fear as they stopped at the steps of the town hall.

People screamed. Husbands hid behind wives.

"It's all right!" Alma said. "Look! Star Bear wasn't sent to hurt us. I found him in the forest. He is gentle and loyal. He's my friend!"

Alma spotted her uncle in the crowd. He stared at her. Then he shook his head and looked away. For a moment all was silent.

Then the mayor appeared.

"Get that beast!" he yelled. "Kill it!"

"No!" Alma cried.

The townspeople roared. They shook their fists.

A nearby hunter raised his bow.

"Run, Star Bear!" Alma shouted.

Townspeople dove out of their way as they
sped through the streets. They did not stop
until they were deep inside the forest.

When at last they were sure no one had
followed them, Alma got down from Star
Bear's back and cried.

"What will we do now?" she asked. "We can't
go back."

Star Bear's nose pointed up. He sniffed the air.

"The mountains," Alma said. "Of course."

The townspeople feared the mountain settlers.
But they had feared the forest and Star Bear,
and they had been wrong. Perhaps they were
wrong about the mountains, too.

The higher they climbed,
the colder it became.

So Alma and Star Bear
set off.

Alma shivered as it
began to snow.

Suddenly, Star Bear stopped. He looked up the mountain, where something galloped towards them. Alma gasped. It looked like a giant, hairy monster.

But when the thing came to a stop, Alma saw it was just a boy. And he was riding a tiger!

The mountain boy wasn't covered in fur
like Alma's uncle had said the settlers were.
He was wrapped in a fur sweater to
keep warm!

"Who are you?" Alma asked.

"I'm Tully," the boy said. "And this is Comet. Who are you?"

"I'm Alma, and this is Star Bear. We come from the forest town, but we can't go back there. We were hoping the mountain settlement would take us."

The boy shook his head. "We just came from there," he said. "I found Comet after the forest was destroyed. She needed a new home, but the settlers thought she was sent by your town to destroy us."

"The townspeople thought Star Bear was sent by the settlement to destroy *us*!" Alma exclaimed.

"Is that why they built that fence?" Tully asked, frowning.

Alma nodded sadly.

"I wish our people would talk to each other," said Tully. "Maybe if they did, they would understand that they don't need to be afraid."

"The people in my town won't listen," said Alma.

"Nor mine," said Tully, "which is why we have to find somewhere else. Because I'm not leaving Comet."

"And I'm not leaving Star Bear."

"Come on," Tully said. "I know a path that leads to the other side of the mountains."

He and Comet set off. Alma's heart beat faster as she and Star Bear followed. "I didn't know there *was* another side of the mountains," she whispered. "The world must be a very big place, Star Bear."

On and on they walked, farther than
Alma ever knew was possible. They
waded through white rivers and
crossed golden prairies.

When Tully and Alma grew tired, Comet
and Star Bear carried them on their backs.
And when they were done walking for the
day, Tully and Alma picked the thorns and
pebbles from the animals' paws.

At last they saw in the distance a great city where everything was black and gray.

"Even the air is gray," Alma said.

"And greasy," Tully added, making a face.
"I can taste it on my tongue."

As they grew nearer, Comet's orange stripes
turned black. A dark cloud of soot hid Star
Bear's white star, too.

When they reached a grove just outside the city, they stopped. "You and Comet wait here," Alma said to Star Bear. "Tully and I will see if we are welcome."

Together she and Tully crossed the bridge leading over a river that circled the city. They came to a gate. A guard stood behind it.

"What do you want?" she asked.

"We need a place to live," said Tully.

Alma was looking past the guard into the city. The people had skin that had turned gray. Some of them looked up at her and scowled.

"Go away!" shouted one.

"There's no room here," said the guard. "We have enough of you already."

Alma hung her head and turned away.

"Who do you think she meant by 'you'?" asked Tully. "You're the only you, and I'm the only me, and she doesn't even know us."

Alma shrugged. She was too hungry and tired to think.

They returned to Comet and Star Bear and set off again. On and on they walked, until the trees turned to bush and the ground gave way to sand. The air grew hot and dry. So did Alma's throat. But there was no river or pool to be found.

"Look!" said Tully finally. "A town!"

Up ahead Alma saw a chain of cheerful houses. They looked much more welcoming than the gray city.

At the first house, they found a girl sitting on the porch. Next to her lay a scrawny wolf.

"Hello," Alma said. She told the girl their names. "We are looking for food and water and a place to stay."

The girl smiled sadly. "I'm Olive," she said. "We have only one well, and the city dwellers have polluted it. You'll get sick if you drink from it."

"Why don't you leave?" Alma asked.

"My brothers moved to the city," said Olive, stroking her wolf. "Lots of people did. Now the dwellers don't want us there anymore."

"That's not right," said Alma, shaking her head. The city dwellers had destroyed Olive's home, and now they were turning her people away.

"What's beyond the desert?" asked Tully.

"Only a forest," said the girl. She bit her lip. "Other children have passed by with their animals, too. They go and never return."

"You should come with us," Alma said. "Sometimes you're only afraid of something because you don't understand it yet."

The girl shook her head. "I am not afraid," she replied. "This is my home. We were happy here."

Alma understood. If she ever found a place where she really belonged she would never want to leave, either.

Tully and Alma turned to go.

"Wait!" said Olive. She held up a basket. "My brothers send food for us. Please, take some. And take Sparrow, my wolf. There isn't enough for him here. With you he will have a chance."

They each ate a crust of bread while Olive hugged Sparrow and whispered in his ear.

"We will take care of him," promised Alma. The wolf took one last look at the girl and trotted to Alma's side.

The forest was darker than any
Alma and Tully had crossed.
The trees had branches like old,
twisted arms. They grew close
together and their leaves made
a heavy canopy.

"I don't like it in here," Alma
said to Star Bear. She was very
thirsty now, and with every step
she felt more tired.

The trees grew thicker. Tully and
Alma walked between them one at
a time. Comet's eyes darted around
the forest. Sparrow cried.

Finally the trees were too close for
Star Bear to go any farther. "What
do we do?" Tully asked. "We can't
go back!"

Alma thought of how far they had traveled. She thought of the mayor's red face and her uncle turning away from her. It seemed so long ago that he had scolded her for climbing up the tree in their yard.

Alma gasped. That was it!

"We don't go forward, Tully," she cried. "We go up!"

"We'll help each other," said Tully, nodding.

Alma led the way up the nearest tree. Sparrow trembled as Star Bear nudged him to the first branch, then the next. Comet stuck close to Tully.

Alma felt as though they were in a very dark, very narrow tunnel, which seemed to go on forever.

Finally she saw a tiny light above.

"Keep going!" she said.
"We're almost there!"

The light grew larger and brighter. Suddenly hands were reaching down and pulling Alma out of the darkness.

Star Bear and Sparrow appeared next. They came to sit by Alma while a boy helped Tully and Comet up. Alma saw they had reached the top of the tree canopy. It was so thick that it created a second green ground.

In the bright distance, Alma could see tables full of food. Other children were swinging in hammocks and playing with animals.

"Welcome!" said a girl. A boy handed a
wooden cup of water to her and Tully.

"It's rainwater," said the boy as he gave
each of the animals their own bowl. Alma
stroked Star Bear's fur as he lapped up the
cool drink.

"What is this place?" Tully asked.

"The horizon," said the girl.

"Can we stay here?" asked Alma.

"Everyone who finds this place is welcome," said the boy, "because we were all brought here by the same things."

"What things?" Tully asked.

"Courage," said the boy. "And love. That's what connects us all."

For a moment, Alma wondered what the boy meant. Then she looked over at Star Bear, and found that she knew. It was her love for Star Bear that made her leave her town. In return, he had given her the courage to keep going all this way. Perhaps, Alma thought, love and courage were often the very same thing.

The boy smiled. "Come and meet everyone – all your new neighbors!"

He and the girl ran off.

Alma turned to Tully. "I think we were always neighbors," she said. "All of us. We just couldn't see it before."

Tully nodded. "But up here there are no fences or mountains or rivers to stop us from seeing each other."

"Do you think Olive will come one day?" Tully asked.

"I don't know," said Alma. Part of her hoped not. She hoped something would change, and Olive's town would become a happy place again.

But if it didn't, she hoped Olive would come. Then she and Sparrow would find each other again.

"Come on," said Tully. "Let's go and meet the others."

He, Sparrow, and Comet ran off to where the children were gathering.

But Alma stayed a moment longer, snuggled up next to Star Bear. All this time she had wondered where she belonged. She had traveled the world to find it. But she had been there all along. She belonged right next to Star Bear. They belonged *together*.

Alma looked around. The coral sun was setting. Soon stars would glitter in the sky, and she and Star Bear would count them until they fell asleep. They would probably never be able to count them all.

She wrapped her arms around the bear's neck and he tickled her with his wet nose.

"Welcome home, Star Bear,"
she said.